EVERYBODY
BRINGS NOODLES

by Norah Dooley

illustrations by Peter J. Thornton

M Millbrook Press/Minneapolis

Millbrook Press
A division of Lerner Publishing Group, Inc.
241 First Avenue North
Minneapolis, Minnesota 55401 USA

For reading levels and more information, look up this title at www.lernerbooks.com.

Library of Congress Cataloging-in-Publication Data

Dooley, Norah.
    Everybody brings noodles / by Norah Dooley ; illustrations by Peter J. Thornton.
       p.   cm.
    Summary: The block party was Carrie's idea, but when it arrives she can only think about two things: the talent show and the delicious noodle dishes from many countries that her neighbors are bringing.
    ISBN 978-0-87614-455-8 (lib. bdg. : alk. paper)
    ISBN 978-1-57505-185-7 (EB pdf)
    [1. Parties—Fiction. 2. Neighborhood—Fiction. 3. Noodles—Fiction. 4. Cookery, International—Fiction.] I. Thornton, Peter J., ill. II. Title.
PZ7.D7265 Ew 2002
    [Fic]—dc21   2001001636

Manufactured in the United States of America
11-52460-6659-1/12/2022

BANG! I woke with a start. It was hot. I was late for something, but what was it?

Bang! Bang! More firecrackers and some hammering. Looking outside, I could see Dad and my brother Anthony working on a stage. The street was closed. It was the day of the block party!

I fell back onto my bed. The block party was my idea, but I had had no idea how much work it was going to be. Lots of people were helping, but I ended up being in charge of a bunch of things. I reached for my list. It was long and crumpled. Just about everything was checked off. I'd given up trying to figure out what to do for the talent show a few days ago, so I'd crossed it off the list. But I wish I was doing something.

I went looking for some breakfast and my mom. She wasn't in the kitchen. But basil leaves were soaking in a bowl of cold water, and water boiled and bubbled in the big pasta pot.

"Mom?" I called.

"I'm in the yard, Carrie," Mom answered from where she was clipping more basil leaves.

I walked out into a day that felt like a sweaty sock. "Good morning!" Mom said brightly.

I just stared at the basil.

Mom looked at me hard. "This is block party day. Aren't you excited?"

"Oh, I don't know," I said, crushing some leaves.

"You don't?" She looked at me again. "Is something bothering you?"

"Well, I wish I was doing something for the talent show," I said.

She gave me a hug and a wink. "I wouldn't worry about that if I were you. You're doing a ton of work anyway."

What a big help she is, I thought.

"Do you want breakfast?"

"Could I have some pasta?" I asked. My most favorite food in the whole world is pasta—any shape, any kind. I could eat it three times a day, seven days a week.

After a bowl of pasta with butter—what my mom calls comfort food—I helped make pesto sauce for the party. Some people think it's kind of weird to have a green sauce on spaghetti noodles, but I love the basil, cheese, pine nuts, and olive oil that go in it.

I took out my list again. "I still have to get the tablecloths," I said, checking off the tables and chairs I'd gotten last night.

"Fine," said Mom. "We'll be setting up the food at this end of the street." She waved me a kiss.

"Good afternoon!" said Dad. "What, up so early? Ready to help, Monkeyface?"

"Dad! I have a zillion things to do!" I said, waving my list at him. Besides, Anthony and my little sister Anna had a line of kids waiting for turns to use Dad's big hammer.

A screen slid open above me, and bubbles came floating down.

"Carrie!" called a small voice. It was Mei-Li. She waved her bubble wand at me. "Come. Come. Mother wants you."

Tablecloths could wait. Up on the third floor of the six-family building, our friend Mrs. Hua held her huge wok. She lifted the cover to show me her beautiful yellow sesame noodles. Then she handed the wok to me, explaining that she had to work today. "But," she said, "Mei-Li will come to the party with Father."

As I carried the wok downstairs, I bumped into John and Anna-Eleni Stephanopolis. They are in college, and I don't get to see them much anymore.

"Yo!" said John. "Will there be water balloons like you wanted?"

"Yes," I said. "I got Noel at the store on the square to give balloons—and popsicles, too. Could you get them and bring them to my mom or Mrs. Tran?"

"No problem," said John.

We stepped from the cool of the hallway into a wall of heat. Whoa, was it hot!

"What are you doing for the show?" asked Anna-Eleni.

"What are you guys bringing for food?" I changed the subject.

"This is orzo. Mom and I made it," said Anna-Eleni.

"It's like a Greek noodle thing," said John, as he walked toward the corner store.

"But different," said Anna-Eleni. "The noodles look like rice but taste like pasta. My mom puts olives and cucumber in it with some feta cheese."

"Cool! I'll have to try it."

The wok was heavy, so I walked faster.

"Hey Carrie! Wait!" It was my next door neighbor, Tam Tran. She was out of breath and waving a T-shirt in front of her.

"Carrie, want to see what we're wearing for our dance? We made these with fabric paint."

"Wild," I said, looking at her black shirt with a metallic design.

"Yo, Tam!" interrupted Fendra Diaz from her back porch. Tam, Fendra, and Fendra's brother Tito are my best friends on the whole block. "Tam, get yourself over here. We need to practice!" said Fendra.

Tam changed her walk to a hip-hop step as she made her way over to the Diazes' house. I wish I could dance as well as my friends.

"What did you and Tito make for food?" I asked Fendra. She's learned a ton about cooking from her grandmother in Puerto Rico.

"Abuela's macaroni salad. Tito will bring it down at noon."

"And my mom's making spring rolls," Tam chimed in. "You'll like them, Carrie. They have noodles in them."

"All right! It's going to be my kind of party."

Mrs. Shinzawa was bringing out her folding chairs as I delivered sesame noodles. The Shinzawas just moved to our block last Thanksgiving.

"Is Mr. Shinzawa going to play the flute today?" I asked. He plays with the City Orchestra. I can hear him practice every night.

"Yes, thank you for asking," said Mrs. Shinzawa. "And we are bringing zaru soba, for this day is so hot."

"What's that?"

"Buckwheat noodles in cold broth. I hope you will try it."

"You bet!" I said.

My dad was listening from the stage. He and Mark DeLoach were setting up the sound system. "You could put noodles on cardboard and Carrie would eat them," Dad said.

"No tablecloths yet?" asked Mom. She was cleaning tables with some of the other moms. Madame Bleu looked up from her clipboard. She is our backyard neighbor, and she's in charge of the talent show.

I turned to run up the street once more. "I'll be right back with the tablecloths." At the corner I looked back. It was beginning to look like a party. Grills, tables, chairs, and kids filled the street.

Tito Diaz came running down his steps with a big bowl of macaroni salad.

"Did you get that free ice cream, Carrie?"

"Yep. Will you help me bring it? We'll need your wagon."

"Yes! Just tell me when," said Tito, and he trotted down to the food tables.

I rang Mrs. Max's bell and looked at my list. I crossed off *wagon for ice cream—get Tito's help.*

"Come in, my dear," said Mrs. Max. She walked back to the kitchen. "Come by the fan. A glass of cool water for you?"

"Yes, thank you," I said, blinking my eyes in the cool darkness. "What smells so sweet?"

"Why, that is the kugel I promised you." On the table was a huge pan filled with a baked noodle thing.

"Boy, are there going to be a lot of noodles today."

"That is good?" Mrs. Max sounded worried.

"That is very good. I love noodles!"

"And here also are my old tablecloths. You have worked hard. How is everything on the great day? You are pleased with it all? Yes?"

I picked at the buttery top of the kugel, trying to hide my face. "Oh, I feel so awful!" I was surprised how it popped out of my mouth.

"But why?"

I told her.

"Ahhh, and all your friends are in the show, so you feel bad?" said Mrs. Max, reaching up to pat my shoulder. "Well, I also am not doing my song and dance today." She did a little tap dance that made me laugh, even though a tear wiggled down my cheek.

"Everybody does their part, yes?" she said.

I nodded again.

"For my part, I got up before light to make the kugel in the cool of morning. Besides, somebody has to be audience, no?"

"Yes," I said, wiping my face with the tissue she handed me.

"And you will be audience right next to me?"

"Yes," I said, took out my list and pencil, and crossed off *tablecloths* and *Mrs. Max's kugel*.

"I come later, when the sun is not so hot. Then, I will see your happy face," she said, and she gave my cheek a gentle pinch.

"Thanks, Mrs. Max," I said, giving her a quick hug.

I ran down to the food tables, dodging sprinklers and whooping, "I'm 'being audience' with Mrs. Max," to nobody in particular.

With the tablecloths and flowers from everyone's gardens, the food tables looked awesome. And there were noodles, noodles, and more noodles.

"You could take your stomach on a world tour," said Dad, as he went around again for thirds.

I had two servings of each kind of pasta, from pesto to zaru soba. I was in noodle heaven.

After the sack races and other games, Tito and I went to Toscanini's and wheeled the ice cream back before it all melted. Then Madame Bleu climbed onto the stage to start the talent show. Mrs. Max and I sat near Mom and Dad and Anna, eating our ice cream and watching from Mrs. Max's beach chairs.

Tam and Fendra did their hip-hop dance. Tito did his own original rap song about ice cream. John and Anna-Eleni played duets on their trumpets. When Mr. Shinzawa played Japanese flute music, everybody got really quiet. A cool breeze started to blow as the sun slid down behind the buildings. Dad got up and played with some drummers. Being audience was actually fun.

After the last act, Madame Bleu asked the drummers to play a loud roll, calling for attention. "Time for thank-yous. First of all, let's thank everybody outside the 'family.'" She read from a long list, thanking everyone from the mayor and the police chief to the supermarket and Toscanini's Ice Cream. Toscanini's got the biggest cheer.

Madame Bleu continued. "And inside the 'family,' let's recognize the committee who put this day together! Stand up, you all."

Mom and I stood up together, along with the others on the committee. People clapped, whistled, and yelled, louder than they had for the ice cream.

"Wait," continued Madame Bleu. "Before we dance and hand out sparklers, we have one special person to thank: the one who talks with everybody. She's the one who got us all talking with each other. She shares her talent with us every day. That person is . . . "

"CARRIE!"

Me?

"Go now, my dear," said
Mrs. Max. Mom nodded and
gently pushed me up. Mom was
crying her happy tears. She is *so*
embarrassing sometimes. I didn't
know how to react.

Then Anthony started
everybody chanting "Carr-ie!
Carr-ie! Carr-ie!" until I climbed
onstage with Madame Bleu. She
gave me a big hug. I looked out
at all my neighbors.

What a great day!

What great noodles!

What a great neighborhood!

Recipes

Mom's Pesto Pasta

Pesto can be ground by hand with a stone bowl and mashing stick, called a mortar and pestle. A blender or food processor works just as well, however, and it takes less time.

3 large garlic cloves
salt and pepper to taste
½ cup pine nuts or walnuts
3 cups fresh basil leaves, loosely packed
½–¾ cup extra virgin olive oil
½ cup grated Parmesan cheese
¼ cup grated Romano cheese
1 pound fettuccine or linguine pasta

1. Blend the garlic, salt and pepper, and pine nuts or walnuts until finely chopped.
2. Add the basil to the garlic and nuts in the blender. Slowly pour in the oil. Blend until smooth.
3. Add the cheeses and stir just enough to combine.
4. Boil the noodles according to package directions, drain, and transfer to large bowl.
5. Spoon the sauce over the noodles. Toss and serve.

Mrs. Hua's Yellow Sesame Noodles

1 pound Chinese egg noodles (may substitute spaghetti or linguine)
½ cup dark sesame oil
2 tablespoons sesame tahini (sesame paste)
⅔ cup creamy peanut butter
3 tablespoons white vinegar
1–2 tablespoons hot oil sauce
6 tablespoons sugar
2 large garlic cloves, crushed
1–2 tablespoons fresh ginger, grated
1 cup bouillon broth, vegetable or chicken
1 cup soy sauce
1 large cucumber, peeled and chopped into cubes
1 bunch scallions (green onions), finely minced

1. Boil the noodles according to package directions. In a colander, rinse thoroughly under cold running water. Drain well.
2. Mix the chilled noodles with the sesame oil. Cover to allow the noodles to absorb the sesame flavor.
3. In a blender or bowl, combine the tahini, peanut butter, vinegar, hot oil sauce, sugar, garlic, ginger, vegetable or chicken broth, and soy sauce. Blend or stir until smooth.
4. Combine the sauce, noodles, cucumber, and minced scallions in a large bowl. Toss well and serve.

The Stephanopolises' Greek Orzo Salad

1 pound orzo pasta
⅓ cup virgin olive oil
6–8 ounces feta cheese, crumbled
1 lemon, zest (grated rind) and juice
1 small bunch fresh mint leaves, coarsely chopped
1 teaspoon Greek oregano
½ cucumber, peeled and chopped
15–20 black olives or Greek olives, sliced
3 tablespoons white wine vinegar
1 teaspoon sugar

1. Cook the orzo in salted boiling water until firm and tender to the bite. Drain and transfer to a bowl.
2. Drizzle with the olive oil and stir to separate the grains.
3. Add the crumbled feta, lemon juice, lemon zest, mint, oregano, cucumber, olives, vinegar, and sugar to the orzo.
4. Mix well and serve immediately.

Fendra's Abuela's Macaroni Salad

Pigeon peas are also called gandules, gungo peas, or congo peas. You can buy them in Latin American grocery stores. If you can't find them, substitute one box of frozen green peas, thawed completely.

1 pound elbow macaroni
1 can pigeon peas, drained
1 medium yellow bell pepper, seeded and diced
1 medium red onion, thinly sliced
¼ cup red wine vinegar
1 cup safflower oil
2 teaspoons salt
2 teaspoons sugar
1 teaspoon black pepper
3 tablespoons cilantro, chopped

1. Boil the macaroni according to package instructions. Drain the macaroni, rinse with cold water, and drain again.
2. Combine the cooked macaroni, peas, yellow pepper, and onion in a large bowl.
3. In another bowl, whisk together the vinegar, oil, salt, sugar, and black pepper.
4. Pour the dressing over the salad. Add the cilantro and toss well.
5. Refrigerate for at least 30 minutes, toss again, and serve.

Mrs. Tran's Vietnamese Spring Rolls with Peanut Sauce

Most Asian markets sell rice paper wrappers, and some large supermarkets also carry them. For a new take on this vegetarian recipe, try adding shrimp. Use shrimp that's already precooked, shelled, and deveined.

Spring Rolls

1 cup rice vermicelli pasta
1 medium carrot, grated
1–2 scallions (green onions), finely chopped
1½ cups Chinese cabbage or iceberg lettuce, finely shredded
4–5 tablespoons fresh cilantro, finely chopped
8 sheets rice paper wrappers
16 medium precooked shrimp (optional)

1. Soak the rice vermicelli in very warm water until soft, about 5-10 minutes. Rinse under cold water and drain well.
2. Combine the carrot, green onion, cabbage, and cilantro. Add the noodles and toss well.
3. Fill a large platter with warm water. To soften the rice paper wrappers, carefully dip one sheet at a time into the warm water for a few seconds.
4. Spoon a tablespoon or two of the noodle mixture onto the center of a softened wrapper, about 2 inches from each end.
5. If using shrimp, place 2 shrimp per roll on the noodle mixture.
6. Fold in the ends first, then tightly roll up the wrappers. Serve with peanut sauce.

Peanut Sauce

¼ cup hoisin sauce
2 tablespoons creamy peanut butter
1½ teaspoons tomato paste
1 teaspoon sugar
⅓ cup water
1 teaspoon safflower or corn oil
1½ teaspoons minced garlic
¼–½ teaspoon crushed red pepper flakes

1. In a small bowl, mix the hoisin sauce, peanut butter, tomato paste, sugar, and water.
2. In a small saucepan, heat oil over high heat about 20 seconds. Add the garlic and crushed red pepper. Stir-fry about 10 seconds, until fragrant.
3. Stir in the peanut butter mixture and cook over medium heat for 3 to 4 minutes.
4. Serve sauce warm or at room temperature with spring rolls.

The Shinzawas' Zaru Soba

Kombu seaweed, or kelp, is available in Asian grocery stores or health food markets. Asian cooks warn against rinsing the seaweed, which depletes the flavor. Instead, simply wipe the kombu with a dry cloth.

16 ounces soba noodles (buckwheat noodles)
2 tablespoons dark sesame oil
2 tablespoons white sesame seeds
1 cup water
1 piece kombu
½ cup Japanese soy sauce
½ cup mirin or sweet sherry
1 scallion (green onion), chopped
salt or sugar to taste

1. Cook the noodles in boiling water until tender. (Cook about 4 minutes for dried soba, 2 minutes for fresh.) Rinse in cold water to chill the noodles. Drain well.
2. Transfer noodles to a bowl. Toss with sesame oil and sesame seeds.
3. In a small saucepan, bring the water to a boil and drop in the kombu. Boil for 3 to 4 minutes. Remove the kombu and save the broth.
4. Stir the soy sauce, mirin, scallion, and salt or sugar into the kombu broth. Cool sauce to room temperature.
5. Pour sauce over the noodles. Toss well and serve.

Mrs. Max's Kugel

This dish, although on the sweet side, is traditionally served with dinner.

1 pound egg noodles
4 eggs, beaten
1 pint cottage cheese
1 pint sour cream
1½ sticks butter or margarine
salt, to taste
½ cup golden raisins
¼ cup sugar
1 cup cornflakes
1–2 teaspoons cinnamon

1. Preheat oven to 350 degrees.
2. Boil the egg noodles until al dente. Drain.
3. Blend together the eggs, cottage cheese, sour cream, butter, and salt. Mix in the noodles and raisins. Transfer to a 9 × 13-inch baking dish.
4. In a small bowl, mix together the sugar, cornflakes, and cinnamon. Sprinkle over the noodle mixture.
5. Bake for 1 hour. Serve hot or at room temperature.